What a beautiful day!

Ladybug was chatting with her friend Butterfly while sweeping the front porch. The Babybugs were coming home from school.

The dust falling off the porch tickled Frog's nose.

Frog let out an earth shattering sneeze that scared the daylights out of Ladybug!

A terrified Butterfly flew away as quickly as she could.

Rabbit looked at Butterfly and thought: *Hey, wait a second! No one is faster than me!*

Rabbit chased after Butterfly into the backyard next door where Nathan, Kyle, and Phoebe were playing soccer.

Mom and Dad were waltzing the afternoon away!

Rabbit leaped up to catch Butterfly.

BOOM-CRASH!

Rabbit slammed into Phoebe. And into the air she went!

Everyone looked on helplessly as Phoebe flew higher and higher . . .

... and crash landed on a cloud!

It was no ordinary cloud! It had a pond, a throne, cupboards, and trees.

Who are these two curious looking creatures? thought Phoebe.

"Welcome to our home," said the fuzzy one as she helped Phoebe to her feet. "I am Cloud and that is Squeeky Wailer and we are delighted that you dropped by!"

Cloud took Phoebe by the hand and led her towards the edge of the cloud. What a wonderful sight it was from up there!

"There is my school!" said Phoebe. "And grandma's house... and over there is my house!" she said, looking for them in the town below.

Phoebe's face fell when she spotted her brothers, mom, and dad.

"Why are you sad?" asked Cloud.

"I miss my family," said Phoebe.

"Don't you worry," said Cloud. "I will come up with a swell spell!"

*Finger, finger, on my hair
Turn me into a giant Eclair!*

And just like that Cloud morphed into a humongous, delicious, mouth-watering, chocolate covered eclair.

"Oops, not that!" said Cloud, snapping her fingers to undo the spell. "Let me try again."

Finger, finger on my temple
Think of an idea that works and is simple!

"Eureka! I've got it!" exclaimed Cloud. "Squeeky, can you please call Wind?"

"Wind! Wiiiiiind!" wailed Squeeky!

Squeeky was shrill. Squeeky was loud. And Squeeky sounded awful.

But Squeeky got the job done!

As Wind started to blow, Cloud pointed to Phoebe's house and said: "Wind, can you please take us over there?"

Wind obliged and off they went.

Squeeky put on a poncho. He found the wind a bit chilly.

Wind carried them right up to Phoebe's house. Everyone waved to each other.

Rabbit couldn't contain his excitement and was running around like crazy!

But how was Phoebe going to get home? "This is way too high up for me to jump down!" she said.

"Don't you worry," said Cloud. "I will come up with a swell spell!"

Finger, finger, on my nose
Spray me with a garden hose!

Phoebe found a drenched Cloud so very funny!

"Oops, not that!" said Cloud, snapping her fingers to undo the spell. "Let me try again."

Finger, finger on my temple
Think of an idea that works and is simple!

"Eureka! I've got it!" exclaimed Cloud. "Squeeky, can you please call Bird?"

"Bird! Biiiiird!" wailed Squeeky!

Squeeky was shrill. Squeeky was loud. And Squeeky sounded awful.

But Squeeky got the job done!

A flock of birds in the shape of the letter V was flying to a distant land.

One bird flew over to find out what the fuss was all about.

"Bird, can you please help us and take Phoebe down to her family?" asked Cloud.

"Sure thing! Always happy to help," said Bird.

But when bird turned around and looked at Phoebe, she almost had a heart attack!

"She is... she is... sooooo biiiig," said Bird!

Cloud kneeled down and gently touched Bird. Magically, its plain colors changed into yellow, red, blue, and gold!

"Whoa, I am Super Bird! I could carry Phoebe on one feather!" boasted Bird.

But Phoebe had her doubts. "Bird is so small," she said, "what if I fall off when she is carrying me?"

"Don't you worry," said Cloud. *Cool!* thought Phoebe. *Another silly spell?* And sure enough, it was!

Finger, finger, on my eye
Take me to a time gone by!

A time portal opened up and Cloud was playing with real dinosaurs inside it. Phoebe almost fell over in surprise!

"Oops, not that!" said Cloud, snapping her fingers to undo the spell. "I am done with spells!"

She went over to her cupboard and brought two bottles. One said "Shrinkaree" and the other said "Biggeree."

She told Phoebe what to do.

Phoebe opened *Shrinkaree*.

Out came a tiny lightning bolt and zapped her on her head (it didn't hurt, if you were wondering).

And Phoebe began to shrink, shrink, shrink . . . until she was tiny.

Phoebe thanked Cloud and Squeeky Wailer for their help. "It was wonderful having you here," said Cloud.

Phoebe climbed onto Bird and they zoomed back to the ground.

Wheeeeeeeee!

Meanwhile, Nathan and Kyle were busy thinking of ways to save their sister.

Nathan wanted to go up in a hot air balloon to rescue Phoebe. Kyle wanted to fly up with a jet pack.

No one noticed Bird and Phoebe in the backyard.

Once they were safely on the ground, Phoebe opened *Biggeree*. Out came a tiny lightning bolt and zapped Phoebe on her head.

She started to get bigger, bigger, bigger ... and jumped off Bird before she got too big!

"Phew!" thought Bird.

"Hey guys, I am over here!" Phoebe called out to her family.

Were they surprised to see her!

Everyone was so happy! Time for a group hug!

"Thank you for bringing Phoebe back!" said Mom and Dad to Bird.

As Bird flew away to join her flock, the gold, blue, red, and yellow colors fell as gold dust on Nathan and Kyle.

Rabbit looked at Bird and thought: *Hey, wait a second! No one is faster than me!*

Rabbit chased after Bird.

Everyone yelled in unison:

Look before you leap, Rabbit!

Made in the USA
Monee, IL
05 March 2025

13536235R00019